THE VERY HUNGRY CATERPILLAR

by Eric Carle

PUFFIN

PUFFIN BOOKS

Published by the Penguin Group: London, New York, Australia, Canada, India, Ireland, New Zealand and South Africa
Penguin Books Ltd, Registered Offices: 80 Strand, London WC2R 0RL, England

puffinbooks.com

First published in the USA by The World Publishing Company, Cleveland and New York, 1969
Published in Great Britain by Hamish Hamilton Ltd 1970
Published in Picture Puffins 1974
Published in this edition 2014

001

Copyright © Eric Carle, 1969
All rights reserved

Printed in China

British Library Cataloguing in Publication Data
A CIP catalogue record for this book is available from the British Library

ISBN: 978–0–723-29785-7

Eric Carle's name and his signature logotype are trademarks of Eric Carle

To find out more about Eric Carle and his books, please visit eric-carle.com
To learn about The Eric Carle Museum of Picture Book Art, please visit carlemuseum.org

For my sister Christa

In the light of the moon
a little egg lay on a leaf.

One Sunday morning the warm sun came up and – pop! – out of the egg came a tiny and very hungry caterpillar.

He started to look for some food.

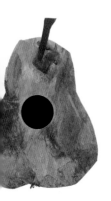

n Tuesday
ate through
o pears,
t he was
ll hungry.

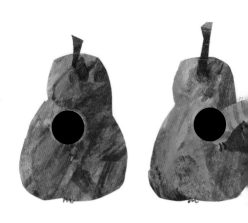

n Wednesday
 ate through
ree plums,
t he was still
ngry.

n Thursday
e ate through
ur strawberries,
t he was still
ungry.

n Friday
e ate through
ve oranges,
ut he was still
ungry.

On Saturday
he ate through
one piece of
chocolate cake, one ice-cream cone, one pickle, one slice of Swiss cheese, one slice of salami,

one lollipop, one piece of cherry pie, one sausage, one cupcake, and one slice of watermelon.

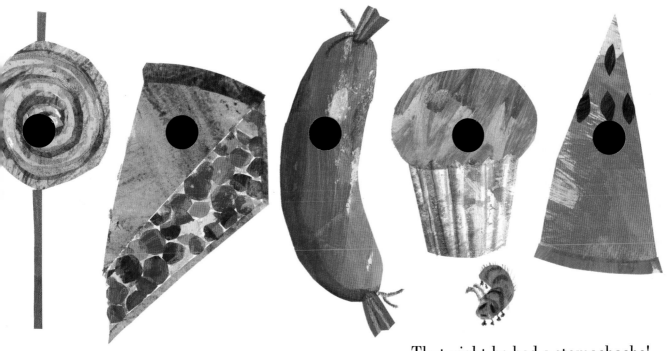

That night he had a stomachache!

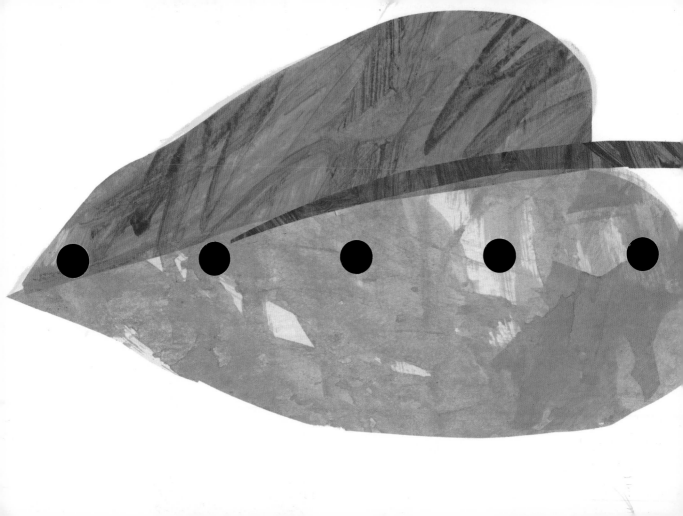

The next day was Sunday again.
The caterpillar ate through
one nice green leaf,
and after that he felt
much better.

Now he wasn't hungry any more – and he wasn't a little caterpillar any more.
He was a big, fat caterpillar.

He built a small house, called a cocoon, around himself. He stayed inside for
more than two weeks. Then he nibbled a hole in the cocoon, pushed his way out and . . .

he was a beautiful butterfly!

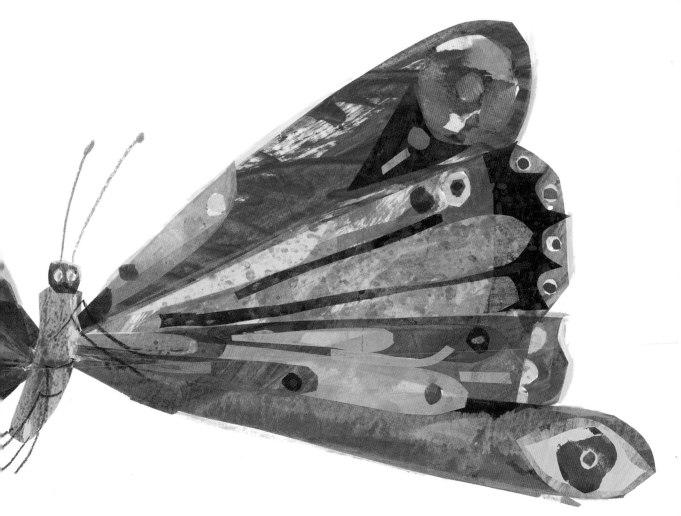